Robert Schumann
And Mascot Ziff
Study Guide

By
Judy Wilcox

Elyria, OH

Robert Schumann and Mascot Ziff
Study Guide

ISBN 10: 1-933573-07-4
ISBN 13: 978-1-933573-07-6
© 2006 by Zeezok Publishing

Published by:
Zeezok Publishing
PO Box 1960
Elyria, OH 44036

www.Zeezok.com
1-800-749-1681

Map of the major cities Schumann visited

Schumann's World and Place in Musical History

Middle Ages	450 – 1450
Renaissance	1450 – 1600
Baroque	1600 – 1750
Classical	1750 – 1820
Romantic *(Robert Schumann 1810 – 1856)*	**1820 – 1900**
20th Century or New Music	1900 – Present

1810 – 1818

1810

Robert Schumann is born in Zwickau, Germany, on June 8. Napoleon is at the height of his power. Simon Bolivar emerges as a major figure in South American politics. Frederic Chopin of Poland is born.

Napoleon invades Russia, but retreats six months later. **1812**

1816

Robert starts school at a small, private day school where he learns the rudiments of music. R.T. Laennec invents the stethoscope. Argentina declares its independence. The American Bible Society is founded.

Schumann begins lessons with Herr Johann Kuntsch, organist at Marienkirche in Zwickau. Border between Canada and U.S. is agreed upon (the 49th parallel). Chile proclaims its independence. Karl Marx, political philosopher and socialist, is born. **1818**

Chapter One

Reading Comprehension Questions

1. For what major event were the people of Zwickau preparing at the start of this chapter?
   - The passage of French soldiers, the Emperor Napoleon, and his empress on the way to Russia, p. 12.
2. What did Robert's father do for a living?
   - He was a book printer and seller, and author as well, pp. 14, 18.
3. What were some of the ways August Schumann, Robert's father, showed love and attention to his five children?
   - He read aloud to them before bed, taught them other languages, shared his coin collection with them, and encouraged Robert in his music, pp. 18, 21.
4. Why did Robert's mother, Johanna Schumann, not really want Robert to become a musician?
   - She believed there was no money in music, p. 22.
5. Even as a youth, when Robert was troubled or distressed, in what did he seek comfort?
   - In music, p. 23.

Character Qualities

Leadership (pp. 14–15) – Early on, Robert demonstrated his ability to organize groups and work with or lead others. He coordinated his friends, young and old, for a make-believe drama of soldiers marching to Russia, with himself as Napoleon.

Attentiveness (pp. 15, 18, 20–21) – Robert listened carefully to the music of the French army as it marched through Zwickau, and he watched attentively the actions of the emperor so that he could mimic him perfectly in play. He was able to recite long poems his father taught him, attentive to every line. And Robert attended to the instructions of his first piano teacher so well that he was able to play entire compositions perfectly in one day.

Emotional (pp. 13, 23) – While extreme variation in emotion is not often something we would recommend in most individuals, in Robert's case his emotional elements in his music stand out as what made him unique as a composer. From his excitement over the grandeur of the emperor and empress passing through Zwickau, to his weeping at not being able to "find" the notes for his music, Robert showed a life of deep emotion. Moreover, he consistently sought solace in music during those emotionally charged moments.

Tidbits of Interest

Page 9 – Zwickau, pronounced [tsvik'ou], is in the region of Saxony in east central Germany along the Mulde River. It is situated at the foot of the Erzgebirge (or Ore) Mountains that form the old border between Saxony and Bohemia (modern-day Czech Republic). Coal and iron have been mined from those mountains since the Middle Ages.

Page 10 – Robert was born June 8, 1810, to Friedrich August Schumann and Johanna Schnabel Schumann. He had three older brothers and one older sister: Edouard (1797), Carl (1801), Julius (1805), and Emilie (1807).

Page 12 – Robert was born at the height of Emperor Napoleon Bonaparte's dazzling career.[1] Robert would have been only about two years old when he witnessed the French troops marching through Zwickau on the way to Russia. Napoleon Bonaparte commenced his invasion of Russia on June 23, 1812, and by the time he retreated in November from the hard-fought invasion of Moscow, a stunning 570,000 French soldiers had been lost. Some 400,000 Russian military casualties, plus several hundred thousand Russian civilian casualties, had also occurred during this deadly invasion. Even so, Russia considered it a victorious defensive; Mother Russia had caused Napoleon to retreat! The Empress at this time was Napoleon's second wife, the Archduchess Marie Louise of Austria, whom he had married in 1810. She remained with him until his death.

Pages 14, 18 – August Schumann, Robert's father, was a publisher, journalist, novelist, and bookseller who gave his children a good interest in literature and foreign languages.[2] August sympathized from the start with Robert's inclination toward music.[3] Robert is also described as having been an alert, imaginative, and curious boy.[4]

Page 19 – By the age of six, Robert began playing and composing at the piano.[5]

Page 21 – Robert began music lessons with Herr Kuntsch in 1818. Johann Gottfried Kuntsch was the organist of Zwickau's Marienkirche and first instructed Robert in the rudiments of piano and organ playing. Kuntsch's manner was simple but formal, and he had difficulty controlling his temper when his pupils seemed especially stupid, sometimes boxing their ears or spanking their hind quarters with a blackthorn switch.[6]

Page 22 – Johanna Schumann was two years older than her husband, and she was not as sympathetic toward Robert's musical interests as was August Schumann. A family friend described her as "kind, but easily fired to blaze up in anger. Nonetheless, Robert regarded her as a paragon of all the virtues..."[7] She did not want Robert going into music because she called it "the breadless art."[8]

Page 23 – Robert Schumann was part of the Romantic musical movement, which differed from the Classical movement in that it moved from objectivity and epic works to subjectivity and personal experience.[9] Schumann and his music seem almost inseparable. His music is poetical, emotional, and moody: the very qualities that defined his own life. His music often sets moods with pictures through the notes that do not use a definite event or concrete piece of imagery, or even follow definite rules, but the notes express an emotion or frame of mind.[10]

1819 – 1821

1819 — Clara Wieck is born.

Robert withdraws from private
school and moves to the Zwickau
Lyceum (where he studied until
1828). Revolution occurs in Spain,
forcing King Ferdinand VII to
restore the Constitution of 1812.
The "Missouri Compromise" is
reached, with Maine entering the
Union as a free state and Missouri
as a slave state. Florence
Nightingale is born.

1820

Robert starts directing a school
band. Napoleon dies. Michael
Faraday discovers the fundamentals
of electromagnetic rotation. Simon
Bolivar defeats Spain's army and
ensures Venezuela's independence.

1821

Chapter Two

Reading Comprehension Questions

1. How did Robert lose his cat, Ziff, at the start of this chapter?
    * The cat was swept down the river Mulde as the reluctant captain on Robert's homemade toy boat, pp. 28–29.

2. What was unique about the song Robert composed when Ziff was presumed forever lost?
    * The tune followed no particular melody, and included strange harmonies, p. 30.

3. Father took Robert to a concert in Carlsbad to hear whom? And how did the concert influence Robert?
    * He took Robert to hear the renowned pianist Moscheles, a pupil of Beethoven, pp. 34–35. Robert decides to become a pianist like Moscheles, p. 36.

4. Robert was eleven years old when he gave his first public performance. Do you know for whom he played and why he stood up at the piano?
    * He helped play piano for his music teacher's conducting of the choral piece, "The Last Judgment,", and he stood so his foot could reach the piano pedal, pp. 37–39.

Character Qualities

Sensitivity (pp. 30, 36) – Robert was crushed when he believed that his cat, Ziff, had been "lost at sea" in his toy sailboat on the Mulde, but he used the emotion to write some of his most beautiful melodies. His sensitivity to the beauty of Moscheles's music and performance forever changed Robert's goal in life, causing him to dream of becoming a pianist like the master some day.

Dedication (pp. 29, 37–38) – Robert dedicated hours of his days to playing the piano and composing new tunes. He also worked late into the night, it appears, as his friend and performing partner Piltznig was sleepy and exhausted during practice, but Robert insisted on continuing to work so they could play like Moscheles. He also worked diligently on the accompaniment for Herr Kuntsch's chorale.

Creativity (pp. 30, 32) – Herr Kuntsch admitted that he didn't understand Robert's tunes because they did not follow an established pattern and had strange harmonies, but he knew Robert was gifted in music. Robert's creativity delighted and entertained his listeners.

Tidbits of Interest

Page 27 – The Mulde, a name derived from Old German "Mulda," meaning "dust," is one of the main waterways of Central Europe, originating in the Czech Republic, traversing Germany, and emptying into the North Sea.

Page 33 – This is a perfect chapter for trying a new recipe — and it doesn't even require a fireplace hearth (although reading the chapter next to a cozy fire would be wonderful). Roasted apples can be served as a snack or dessert and have a chewy texture and deepened flavor that are delightful. Use almost any variety of apples, except for red delicious apples, which don't cook as well. Tart varieties of apples become sweeter during the roasting process because the inner moisture evaporates, and the natural sugars in the apple intensify and caramelize.

Roasted Apples

Preheat your oven to 425° F. Spray a ceramic baking dish with nonstick cooking spray. Core the apples, cutting them into fairly large chunks with the *peel on*. (If the apples are peeled, they tend to fall apart.) Place the chunks in a single layer either peel-side down or on their sides in the baking dish. Put the dish into the preheated oven for approximately 30 minutes, or until the apples are done as you like them. When the apples are tender to your touch or when a fork slides easily through the flesh of the apple, remove them from the oven and serve them on a platter or plate. Yummy!

You can also "deglaze" the pan with about ¼ cup of apple juice after you have removed the fruit. Scrape the juice around the dish to catch all the glazed bits that have stuck during the roasting process. You can then drizzle or pour the liquid directly over your roasted fruit.

Page 34 – Carlsbad was no small journey from Zwickau in those days, particularly with a precocious nine-year-old son.[11] It is a village in Bohemia just across the Erzgebirge Mountains along the border.

Ignaz Moscheles (1794–1870) was from Prague, Bohemia. He was one of the greatest pianists of all time, but he was only twenty-five at the point Robert heard him in concert, and he had just recently started his virtuoso career. He had been a pupil of Ludwig van Beethoven, and he was especially fond of playing Bach's works. Robert later expressed his own appreciation for Bach's music when he called Bach "that genius who purifies and gives strength...and whose music seems written for eternity."[12]

Page 37 – Friedrich Piltznig (sometimes spelled Piltzing, depending on the source) was a school friend of Schumann's who played four-handed piano arrangements with Robert. Robert apparently composed these duet arrangements of works by various composers, but especially symphonies and overtures by Haydn.[13]

Page 38 – Robert took part in a musical festival at Herr Kuntsch's church. It is very likely by this time that Kuntsch "found that his pupil had outstripped him, at any rate in practical musicianship, and gave up the futile task of trying to instruct a pupil who could not only argue with the master but prove himself to be in the right."[14] Thus, Kuntsch had complete confidence in Robert's ability to accompany the choir and musicians at the piano, though Robert was only eleven years old.

Page 39 – Robert's favorite instrument remained the piano — whether playing others' works on it, or composing his own music on it. In his piano music, Schumann "shares his most intimate feelings."[15]

1822 – 1830

August Schumann, Robert's father, buys him a grand piano. Brazil becomes independent of Portugal. Franz Liszt makes his piano debut (at age 11). A. J. Fresnel perfects lenses for lighthouses.

1822

1826

Both Robert's father and sister, Emilie, die during this year. Thomas Jefferson dies. Russia declares war on Persia. James F. Cooper's *Last of the Mohicans* is published.

Robert applies at the University of Leipzig and moves there to study law. Uruguay becomes an independent republic separate from Brazil. Franz Schubert, Austrian composer, dies. Alexander Dumas publishes *The Three Musketeers.*

1828

1829

Robert moves to Heidelberg to study law with Professor Thibaut, who is also a musician. Andrew Jackson is inaugurated as the seventh U.S. president. William Booth, founder of the Salvation Army, is born.

Robert determines to give his life to music. Ecuador becomes an independent republic. Simon Bolivar dies. Red Jacket, the Native American leader, dies.

1830

Chapter Three

Reading Comprehension Questions

1. Why did Robert approach crotchety, old Herr Schiffner at the start of this chapter?
    • To ask Herr Schiffner if he could practice on the older man's piano, the best piano in town, pp. 41, 43.
2. Robert organized a small orchestra with his friends. How did his father encourage him?
    • His father surprised him with eight new music stands and a new piano, better than Herr Schiffner's, before their concert, p. 46.
3. In what other area was Robert apparently gifted besides music?
    • Writing. He wrote poems, stories, and biographies on great men that his father published, p. 47.
4. What two family tragedies occurred before Robert left to study law at the university?
    • Robert's sister, Emilie, and his father died, pp. 50, 51.
5. Why did Clara Wieck so impress Robert when he first met the Wiecks?
    • She was only eight years old and was already a piano virtuoso, p. 54.
6. Robert traveled to Frankfort on Easter morning to hear whom? And how did it change his life's course?
    • He heard violin master Paganini play, and because of that concert Robert resolved to pursue music rather than law, pp. 59, 60. He even wrote his mother to beg her consent, p. 61.

Character Qualities

Organized (pp. 43–45) – Robert organized a plan to find a better piano on which to practice for his concert for the people of Zwickau. He then followed that plan and approached Herr Schiffner about practicing on his piano, the best in the village. Robert also coordinated a group of his friends into an orchestra and organized weeks of practice with them to prepare them for a concert.

Intellectual (pp. 47, 51, 53, 58) – While Robert was an emotional man and tending toward the Romantic movement (which focused on emotion), he was an intellectual who was gifted in his writing abilities, as well as his composing talents. After all, Robert was chosen to write some biographies for a set of books his father was publishing on the lives of great men, and Robert enjoyed writing poems and stories. He was studious enough to qualify for law studies at Leipzig's university, and he established a friendship with a law professor in Heidelberg when he moved there. He also was literate enough to feel at ease at Heine's house in Munich. Heine was a premier German poet of the day.

Dreamy (pp. 44, 52, 55, 61) – Most of Robert's dreams revolved around music — from dreaming of playing in an orchestra, to dreaming of becoming a musician in spite of his mother's wishes, to dreaming of studying music under Herr Wieck. Robert also did all he could to make those dreams a reality.

Tidbits of Interest

Page 44 – Robert began directing the school band at age eleven,[16] and his father purchased a grand piano for him by age twelve. Also by the age of twelve, he formed a small orchestra, composed music for voices and instruments set to Psalm 150, and studied the works of Mozart, Haydn, and Weber.

Page 47 – A lyceum is an educational institution equivalent to secondary or high school education in most European countries. During his years at the Zwickau Lyceum Robert wrote some literary sketches for a series on great men of the world that his father was publishing. It was a series that had good success, and it is impressive that Robert's work was included as he was only fourteen at the time of the writing.

Page 48 – Robert and his friends formed a society for the study of German literature. Among its statutes was the notion that "for every man of culture the knowledge of the literature of his country is a duty."[17] However, 1826 was a difficult year for sixteen-year-old Robert. Both his father and his older sister, Emilie, died. For a young man of such a sensitive nature, these were stunning emotional blows. Robert continued school at the Lyceum until moving to Leipzig to study law.

Page 52 – Robert applied to the University of Leipzig in March of 1828, mainly on the insistence of his mother. Leipzig was a musical city as well as a university town. Leipzig's most famous resident had been Bach, who was cantor at a church there from 1723 until his death in 1750. Robert loved the music of J. S. Bach. Leipzig was also the birthplace of composer Richard Wagner in 1813.

Gisbert Rosen was a slightly older law student who had already studied for one year in Leipzig and was transferring to Heidelberg. He and Robert had similar tastes, shared intellectual interests, and developed a close friendship.

Page 53 – Robert's interest in intellectual pursuits and literature is evident in that he "stopped in" Munich on his way to holiday in Heidelberg. Munich is over one hundred miles southeast of Heidelberg — hardly conveniently on the way to the ancient city. Heinrich Heine (1797–1856) was one of Germany's greatest lyric poets. Schumann later composed music for some of Heine's poems. Heine's lyrics were used in more than 3,000 compositions, including works by Mendelssohn, Schubert, and Liszt.

Dr. Ernest Carus and his musical wife, Agnes, had a constant stream of musical people flow through their house. Frau Carus had taken to singing in public with some success, and it was in their home that Robert met numerous musicians of the day, and where he introduced some of his own pieces and poetry.

Pages 54–55 – Herr Friederich Wieck (pronounced [veek]) was one of the greatest piano teachers of the city of Leipzig, and he was well known in Leipzig musical circles. He had trained his daughter Clara, then eight or nine years old, as a piano prodigy. Wieck was said to be rather rude and argumentative about his opinions, but he apparently liked Robert and agreed to teach him the pianoforte. Robert's and Wieck's discussion of works by Franz Schubert, an Austrian composer whose works were not yet well known, would have been taking place near or shortly after Schubert's death. Schubert died very young (1797–1828) of typhoid, before his music gained popularity.

Page 58 – Robert eventually agreed to move from Leipzig to Heidelberg to study law in a city that was less musical. Germany's oldest university, founded in 1386, is located in Heidelberg along the Neckar River. Robert still dreamed of becoming a musician, and his legal studies were neglected. The professor who encouraged Schumann to pursue music was Professor Thibaut, who was a musical celebrity and legal expert who had written a short book attacking the "degeneration of church music in German."[18]

Page 59 – Nicolo Paganini (1782-1840) was an Italian violinist and composer who visited some forty cities in Germany, Bohemia, and Poland from 1828 to 1831. Frankfort is about forty miles from Heidelberg, and Robert wrote his friends of their trip to hear Paganini's Easter evening concert.

Pages 60–61 – By the end of 1830, at twenty years of age, Robert determined to give his life to composition.[19] He told his mother that the study of law froze "the flower of the imagination."[20]

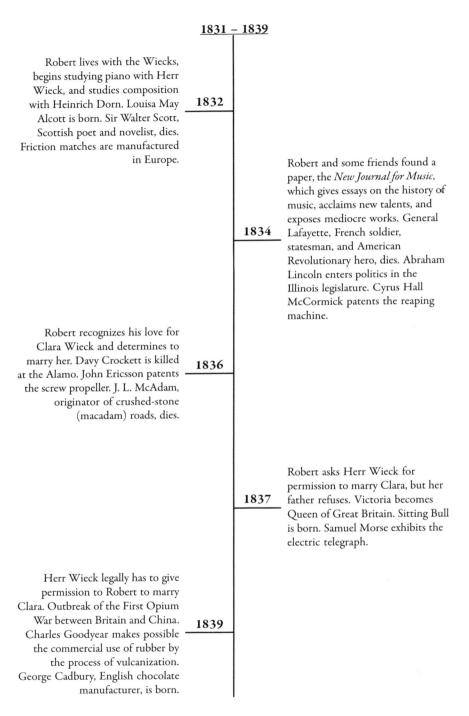

Robert lives with the Wiecks, begins studying piano with Herr Wieck, and studies composition with Heinrich Dorn. Louisa May Alcott is born. Sir Walter Scott, Scottish poet and novelist, dies. Friction matches are manufactured in Europe.

1832

1834

Robert and some friends found a paper, the *New Journal for Music*, which gives essays on the history of music, acclaims new talents, and exposes mediocre works. General Lafayette, French soldier, statesman, and American Revolutionary hero, dies. Abraham Lincoln enters politics in the Illinois legislature. Cyrus Hall McCormick patents the reaping machine.

Robert recognizes his love for Clara Wieck and determines to marry her. Davy Crockett is killed at the Alamo. John Ericsson patents the screw propeller. J. L. McAdam, originator of crushed-stone (macadam) roads, dies.

1836

1837

Robert asks Herr Wieck for permission to marry Clara, but her father refuses. Victoria becomes Queen of Great Britain. Sitting Bull is born. Samuel Morse exhibits the electric telegraph.

Herr Wieck legally has to give permission to Robert to marry Clara. Outbreak of the First Opium War between Britain and China. Charles Goodyear makes possible the commercial use of rubber by the process of vulcanization. George Cadbury, English chocolate manufacturer, is born.

1839

Chapter Four

Reading Comprehension Questions

1. Robert moved in with the Wiecks to study piano under Herr Wieck. What did Herr Wieck promise Robert if Robert studied well?
   - Robert would become a great pianist in three years, p. 65.

2. What did Robert think he needed to do for his right hand, and did it work?
   - He believed he needed to strengthen a weak finger, so he devised a sling for it to keep it up, p. 70. No, it did not work; it weakened it even more and even permanently damaged the finger, pp. 70, 71.

3. Did Robert give up his dream of working with music full-time? If not, what did he determine to do?
   - No, he didn't give up entirely on music; he simply decided to become a composer instead of a musician, p. 72.

4. What did Robert and some of his musician friends decide to start to help all struggling musicians?
   - They decided to publish a music magazine telling of the work and compositions of worthy musicians, p. 74.

5. Initially, Herr Wieck refused to let Robert do something until he won greater honor for himself. What was it?
   - Marry Herr Wieck's daughter, Clara, p. 78.

6. Can you name at least two other composers or musicians that Robert met in this chapter?
   - Clara Wieck, Felix Mendelssohn, Ludwig Schunke, Frederic Chopin, and Franz Liszt.

Character Qualities

Dedicated (pp. 70, 78, 83) – Robert was committed to doing whatever he could to become a better pianist, to the point of ruining his finger on one hand in his efforts to strengthen it. He was also dedicated to Clara Wieck, waiting for nearly two years to gain her father's permission to marry her.

Flexibility (pp. 70, 72) – Ironically, Robert's flexibility was evident in a situation created by a stiff (or inflexible) finger. When Robert permanently damaged one of his fingers through a unique training routine, his goal of becoming a master pianist was snatched from his grasp. While this episode utterly discouraged him, he showed flexibility by changing his life goal without having to give up on music: he became a composer instead of a pianist.

Visionary (pp. 72, 74, 80, 82) – Robert had the vision to experiment with his music, not allowing traditional rules of music to bind his heart's melodies. Fellow composers, such as Franz Liszt, even praised Schumann's compositions as "unequaled." Robert also had a vision for establishing a music magazine to praise and promote unknown musicians, introducing some musicians and some music to the world.

Tidbits of Interest

Page 65 – Robert moved back to Leipzig to begin lessons with Herr Wieck. He actually lived in the Wieck household for almost two years, until 1832. The thought that Robert always liked children is repeated by most of his biographers — perhaps because he himself had been an alert and imaginative boy.

Schumann

Page 68 – Schumann did not enjoy much success during his lifetime. Even his friends did not always understand or appreciate his romanticized, emotional music.[21]

Pages 70–72 – In an effort to strengthen his fourth finger, Robert invented a device for keeping it inactive while practicing. "To his horror, the favored finger tended to retain this artificial position when free."[22] One biographer noted that this finger-ruining shortcut could be considered a providential accident because it turned Robert from performance to composition.[23]

Page 72 – While Robert learned keyboard skills from Herr Wieck, he learned composition and music theory from Heinrich Dorn during the years of 1830 to 1832. Dorn was the conductor of the Leipzig opera and was considered an enterprising, young conductor. Wieck and Dorn "found Schumann a troublesome pupil, because though he worked well, it was irregularly, and to impulse."[24] He frustrated them "by neglecting theory. Also he practiced when he wished, therefore unsystematically, and, as a substitute for more formal studies, read the scores of the best music of all periods."[25]

Robert wrote much of his music with Clara Wieck in mind. Clara was nine years younger than Robert. Her father had initially given her piano lessons as reassurance that Clara was not deaf. When she was young, she could hardly speak, and didn't speak normally until she was eight — when she was already on her way to becoming a world-famous pianist.[26]

Page 74 – In 1834, Robert's writing ability and musical knowledge were combined in a music magazine, the *Neue Zeitschrift für Musik* (*New Journal for Music*), which was filled with reviews of concerts and new music, essays on the history of music, and acclamations of new musicians.

Robert was not a harsh critic because he knew how such criticism hurt, and he did not believe it did any good. His desire was to keep the virtues of works like those by Beethoven and Schubert at the forefront of musical appreciation. His writing labors confirmed the growing fame of such composers as Schubert, Mendelssohn, and Chopin, and introduced Berlioz and Brahms to the world.

Page 75 – Ludwig Schunke (1810–1834) was one of the original four editors of the music magazine, and was a young composer and pianist who had only recently moved to Leipzig from Vienna. He and Robert lived in the same house and became close friends. Schunke introduced Robert to Henrietta and Carl Voigt, amateur musicians and music enthusiasts in Leipzig. It was at the Voigts that Robert met Felix Mendelssohn, who was only one year older than Robert. Felix Mendelssohn-Bartholdy (1809-1847) was among the first interpretive orchestra conductors who used dynamics intentionally and carefully. Schumann once wrote that Mendelssohn was unlike some conductors who threatened to beat up the score, the orchestra, and the audience with their batons. Schumann further admired Mendelssohn's form. "He said he could learn from him (that is, could learn of things by study of his music) for years."[27]

Mendelssohn

Page 76 – Frederic Chopin (pronounced [show' pahn]) was a Polish composer and musician whom Schumann championed from the start. Chopin (1809–1849) is one of the most admired and influential composers for piano. In a review of one of Chopin's works, Robert wrote, "Hats off, gentlemen — a genius!" He later described Chopin's works as "cannons concealed in flowers."[28]

Page 78 – By 1836, Robert recognized his interest in Clara Wieck was love. In 1837, on Clara's eighteenth birthday, he asked Herr Wieck for permission to marry Clara, but Wieck refused, claiming that Robert was too poor and intemperate. According to German law, if after two years Clara's father still withheld his consent, Robert and Clara could resort to legal steps to be permitted to marry.[29]

Pages 79–80 – This C Major Symphony by Franz Schubert had been written near the end of his brief life, and it had never been performed.[30]

Page 81 – Mendelssohn had arrived in Leipzig in 1835 to serve as director of the Gewandhaus concerts. Gewandhaus was a concert hall founded in 1781, and it saw some of its finest days under Mendelssohn's directorship. Musical presentations are still given at the hall regularly.

Leipzig

Page 82 – Franz Liszt (1811–1886) was regarded by many as the greatest pianist of all time, and was the first inventor of impressionism on the piano. Schumann became friends with Liszt, and even performed duets with him at concerts. Robert's own music, however, was still strongly affected by traditional composers like Bach and Beethoven, and he insisted that music should not be vain displays of technical prowess (if playing notes with one's nose can be called prowess) or popularity concerts.

Page 83 – Finally, in 1839, after a two-year wait required by law, Herr Wieck's objections to the marriage and false charges about Robert were dropped, and the engagement between Robert and Clara began.

1839 – 1844

1839

Robert and Clara marry on September 12, the day after her twentieth birthday. (Some sources say the marriage was in 1840.)

1840

Robert composes 150 songs in one year. Queen Victoria of Great Britain marries Prince Albert. Nicolo Paganini, Italian violinist and composer, dies. Claude Monet, French painter, is born.

1841

The Schumanns' first child, a daughter named Marie, is born. Britain proclaims sovereignty over Hong Kong, and New Zealand becomes a British colony. Adolphe Sax, Belgian instrument maker, invents the saxophone.

1843

Robert receives an appointment to teach piano and composition at the newly founded Leipzig conservatory, and he later tours Russia with Clara. Their second child, Elise or Lieschen, is born. Alfred Tennyson publishes *Morte d'Arthur*. Noah Webster, American dictionary compiler, dies. Sequoya, Indian leader who created the Cherokee alphabet, dies.

1844

Robert and Clara's third child, Julie, is born and they move to Dresden. Friedrich Nietzsche, German philosopher, is born. Young Men's Christian Association (YMCA) is founded in England by George Williams.

Chapter Five

Reading Comprehension Questions

1. What had Robert prepared for Clara in honor of her birthday? (There are several possible answers here.)

   • A long birthday walk, birthday music, a special poem, and a new piano with scenes of places she loved set in wood in the piano, pp. 86, 87.

2. What was Robert's primary way of showing his happiness in being married and in having children?

   • He wrote songs. He wrote over one hundred in his first year of marriage, p. 89. He began writing songs for his daughter, Marie, very early in her life, p. 93.

3. When Robert became overworked, what did Clara ask him to do for a holiday?

   • Go with her on tour to Russia while she gave piano concerts, p. 103.

4. Can you provide "proofs" that Robert loved children? (There are several possible answers.)

   • He was eager and joyous to return to his daughters after the Russian tour, p. 106. He was excited about being father to several children over the next few years, p. 111. And he wrote music for a children's composition book upon the arrival of each new baby, p. 112.

Character Qualities

Generous (pp. 86, 93, 103, 111) – Robert loved giving Clara gifts, as demonstrated on her birthday the day before their wedding. He gave her physical, tangible items like a new piano and a new poem, but he also gave her intangible gifts, like time for a long walk with her, which was one of her favorite activities. He wrote music to give to his children. And he gave so much of himself to his music that he actually overworked himself.

Productive (p. 89) – This quality was most evident early on in the Schumanns' marriage. Robert produced over one hundred compositions, including his first symphony, in one year!

Family-oriented (pp. 89, 93, 106, 112) – Life with Clara brought Robert joy, which in turn brought melodies to mind. Robert loved his children very much, and he lovingly wrote music for a special book of compositions for his little ones, with a new composition for each new child. He also delighted in returning home to his family after touring Russia with his wife.

Tidbits of Interest

Page 86 – Clara (Wieck) Schumann loved taking walks, and attempted to do so daily. She attributed her seemingly unending energy to those walks.[31]

Page 87 – Robert and Clara were married September 12, 1839. Robert's art blossomed during this first year of marriage. It was a year in which he composed nearly 150 songs. Schumann once wrote his bride, "I have noticed that my imagination is never so lively as when it is anxiously extended towards you."[32]

Page 90 – Clara Schumann became known as the "Queen of the Piano," and she premiered and championed Robert's music, though it was considered strange or weird in the European musical circles of the time.[33] She was considered the greatest woman pianist of her century.[34]

Page 92 – The Schumanns had eight children in less than sixteen years: Marie (1841), Elise (1843), Julie (1844), Emil (1846), Ludwig (1848), Ferdinand (1849), Eugenie (1851), and Felix (1854).

Page 102 – In 1843, Mendelssohn, who was the head of the newly founded Leipzig conservatory, appointed Schumann to teach piano and composition. Schumann needed the income and the distraction from his own compositions because the writing was causing "nerve exhaustion."[35] Schumann only taught a little more than a year, however, because he was too shy and erratic as a teacher.

Page 103 – As the teacher, you will need to decide how much of the following material you want your children to learn about Schumann. Wheeler is very careful in her descriptions of Robert's final years. It is believed that Robert suffered a nervous breakdown in 1844, so Clara urged him to tour Russia with her while she gave piano concerts. Although this trip was a financial success, it really did not improve Robert's health. It was also during this year that Robert imagined he heard the note A perpetually sounding in his ear. This ear problem, coupled with his high-strung nature, caused him to push himself beyond his physical and mental limits.[36] His final fifteen years of life were difficult as the mental and nervous handicaps worsened.

Page 110 – Robert became even more anxious to remain at home, and in late 1844 the Schumanns thought a complete change of scene would help. So they moved to Dresden, the capital city of the German state of Saxony. Robert lived somewhat in seclusion at first in Dresden, but soon the Schumann home became a place where artists and musicians met.[37]

Page 111 – Among those musical visitors to the Schumann home was Richard Wagner (1813–1883), a German composer, conductor, essayist, opera writer, and music theorist who was the music director (or Kapellmeister) of Dresden. While Robert admired Wagner's courageous, strong, and dramatic composition styles, he considered some of Wagner's works unnatural and strange.[38] It seems ironically apropos that later in the 20th century, Adolf Hitler would like Richard Wagner's compositions above all others.

1845 – 1856

Fourth child, Emil, is born. Brigham Young leads Mormons from Nauvoo City, IL to the Great Salt Lake, Utah. John Deere constructs a plow with steel moldboard. Smithsonian Institution in Washington is founded. Potato famine rages through Ireland.

1846

1848

Fifth child, Ludwig, is born, and Robert's *Album for the Young* is published. Treaty of Guadalupe Hidalgo ends the Mexican-U.S. war. The Communist Manifesto is issued by Marx and Engels. Gold discoveries in California start the gold rush.

Sixth child, Ferdinand, is born. Zach Taylor is inaugurated as twelfth U.S. president. Edgar A. Poe dies. Armand Fizeau, French physicist, measures the speed of light.

1849

1850

The Schumanns moves to Düsseldorf and Robert takes the role of musical director for the city. Zach Taylor dies. Millard Fillmore becomes thirteenth president. Hawthorne's *The Scarlet Letter* is published. Jenny Lind tours America under the management of P. T. Barnum.

Seventh child, Eugenie, is born. Cuba declares its independence. Melville's *Moby Dick* is published. Isaac Singer devises the continuous-stitch sewing machine.

1851

1853

Johannes Brahms enters the Schumann home. Robert accompanies Clara on a tour of Holland. Vincent Van Gogh, Dutch painter, is born. Samuel Colt revolutionizes the manufacture of small arms. Use of first railroad through the Alps.

Eighth child, Felix, is born. Robert's sanity is weakening, and he moves himself to a sanatorium (asylum) in Endenich, Germany. Commodore Perry negotiates first American-Japanese treaty. "War for Bleeding Kansas" between free and slave states begins. Thoreau's *Walden* is published.

1854

1856

Robert dies on July 29. Britain grants self-government to Tasmania. Sigmund Freud, founder of psychoanalysis, is born. "Big Ben" is cast at the Whitechapel Bell Foundry for the British House of Parliament.

Chapter Six

Reading Comprehension Questions
1. Whom did Robert see again in Zwickau who had influenced him early on in his music, even though he had rapped Robert's knuckles when he made mistakes?
   - Herr Kuntsch, p. 117.
2. What were some of the ways Robert showed love and attention to his children? (There are several possible answers.)
   - He wrote music for them, p. 127; he played with them, told them stories, and did dramas with them, p. 130.
3. What young, yet-unknown musician stopped by the Schumanns' house and greatly impressed both Robert and Clara?
   - Johannes Brahms, pp. 134–137.
4. For Clara's birthday and their thirteenth anniversary, what did Robert plan?
   - A birthday picnic, a new piano, and a song from the poem he had given her thirteen years before, p. 139.
5. Where did Robert believe music lived (in every land throughout the whole world)?
   - In the hearts of all little children, p. 141.

Character Qualities

Romantic (pp. 137–139) – Robert remembered Clara's birthday and their anniversary by giving her gifts related to ones he had given her thirteen years earlier, and by serenading her with a song using lyrics from a previously given poem. (Of course, some men would argue that it's not difficult to be romantic and remember both a wife's birthday and an anniversary when they are only one day apart...)

Hospitable (pp. 134, 137) – The Schumanns had numerous musical visitors to their home, even aiding one young musician, Johannes Brahms, by taking him in like a member of the family.

Noble (pp. 130, 137, 141) – Robert looked beyond his own interests or difficulties, and he devoted himself to his children by playing with them and telling stories to them. He encouraged other musicians as much as possible. And Robert promoted music for all people, particularly children, throughout the whole world.

Tidbits of Interest

Pages 115–117 – The Schumanns attended the annual Zwickau summer music festival in 1847. Robert and Clara were greatly honored by the villagers that year.

Page 124 – Richard Wagner was removed as Kapellmeister in Dresden because of his role in the political revolts of 1848–1849. Robert was overlooked as Wagner's successor, so he wished to leave Dresden. The Schumann family then moved to Düsseldorf along the Rhine river when a directorship post became open in that capital city of the German state of North Rhine-Westphalia.

Page 125 – Wheeler says the Schumanns had six children, but history records the names of eight, though only five lived beyond infancy.

Page 127 – Robert's thick book of songs was entitled *Album für die Jugend* (*Album for the Young*), which is a collection of forty-three brief works for children, each based on "sharp little pictures that might appeal to any child."[39]

Page 134 – The Schumann home hosted Liszt, Wagner, and Jenny Lind. Johanna Maria (Jenny) Lind (1820–1887) was from Stockholm, Sweden, and was known as "The Swedish Nightingale." She began as an opera singer and later became a recitalist — including popular songs in her repertoire — as she gave performances throughout Europe, England, and America.

Johannes Brahms (1833–1897) was born in Hamburg, Germany, and was fourteen years younger than Clara (making him more than twenty years younger than Robert). He came to the Schumann house in 1853 and won both Robert and Clara over with his youth, energy, and honesty. A lifelong friendship formed among the three.[40] Brahms also loved children (bringing penny candy to hand out to them), and he enjoyed walks in the woods. He was a perfectionist that Robert announced as the next great composer like Beethoven. In fact, Brahms loved the works of Beethoven, Mozart, and Haydn (endearing him to Robert), and he was inspired by Clara's works — dedicating many of his later works to her. In Robert's final years of mental struggles, when he had withdrawn into himself, he would become especially agitated when Brahms or Clara visited him in the hospital because he could not communicate with them.[41]

The master Joachim, who had encouraged Brahms to stop at the Schumanns' house, was Joseph Joachim (1831–1907), a violinist, conductor, and composer who was mentored by Mendelssohn. He was regarded as one of the most influential violinists of all time. The Schumanns had met Joachim ten years before, when he was a child.

Page 137 – Wheeler gently states that Robert was not strong, but was of a noble mind and heart. Though Schumann remained in Düsseldorf until late 1853 and composed some fifty works while there, he seemed to become lost in a dream world of his own, and was unable to even keep a beat when directing.[42] As his mental suffering continued, he became disinclined to speak, but he enjoyed listening to company or would go to an inn to sit with his face to a wall, whistling softly to himself.[43] Robert Schumann suffered from insanity for his final ten years, living in an asylum in Endenich for the last two years of his life. While he had lucid moments those final two years, he never returned home. He died on July 29, 1856, in Clara's arms, and he was buried in a cemetery in nearby Bonn — with only Clara, Brahms, Joachim, and another musical friend (Ferdinand Hiller) present. At his death, some say the voice of *pure* Romantic music was silenced.

Page 139 – Clara was only thirty-seven when Robert died. She returned to performance work full-time for another forty years in order to provide for her family! In total, she played piano concerts for some sixty years. She continued to play Robert's music, dedicating herself to present Robert's music until he was known and accepted all over Europe and England.[44] As she lay dying at age seventy-seven, she asked her grandson to play Robert's music for her.[45] Her efforts helped ensure that Robert's music would be remembered throughout the whole world, just as Robert had believed that music lived in the hearts of all little children throughout the world.

Endnotes

[1] Herbert Bedford, *Robert Schumann: His Life and Work* (New York: Harper & Brothers, 1925), 31.

[2] Ibid., 35.

[3] Sydney Grew, *Masters of Music* (Boston: Houghton Mifflin Company, No date given), 251.

[4] Jane Stuart Smith and Betty Carlson, *The Gift of Music: Great Composers and Their Influence* (Wheaton, IL: Crossway Books, 1995), 104.

[5] Wallace Brockway and Herbert Weinstock, *Men of Music: Their Lives, Times, and Achievements* (New York: Simon and Schuster, 1950), 293.

[6] Bedford, *Robert Schumann: His Life and Work*, 34.

[7] Ibid., 28.

[8] Smith and Carlson, *The Gift of Music: Great Composers and Their Influence*, 104.

[9] Grew, *Masters of Music*, 249.

[10] Ibid., 261.

[11] Bedford, *Robert Schumann: His Life and Work*, 35.

[12] Smith and Carlson, *The Gift of Music: Great Composers and Their Influence*, 105.

[13] Bedford, *Robert Schumann: His Life and Work*, 36.

[14] Ibid., 36, 37.

[15] Smith and Carlson, *The Gift of Music: Great Composers and Their Influence*, 105.

[16] Brockway and Weinstock, *Men of Music: Their Lives, Times, and Achievements*, 293.

[17] Bedford, *Robert Schumann: His Life and Work*, 37.

[18] Ibid., 61.

[19] Grew, *Masters of Music*, 252.

[20] Bedford, *Robert Schumann: His Life and Work*, 67.

[21] Ibid., 106.

[22] Brockway and Weinstock, *Men of Music: Their Lives, Times, and Achievements*, 295.

[23] Smith and Carlson, *The Gift of Music: Great Composers and Their Influence*, 104.

[24] Grew, *Masters of Music*, 253.

[25] Brockway and Weinstock, *Men of Music: Their Lives, Times, and Achievements*, 294.

[26] Kathleen Krull, *Lives of the Musicians: Good Times, Bad Times* (San Diego: Harcourt, Inc., 1993), 41.

[27] Grew, *Masters of Music*, 258.

[28] Eric F. Jensen, *Schumann* (New York: Oxford University Press, 2001), 117.

[29] Brockway and Weinstock, *Men of Music: Their Lives, Times, and Achievements*, 299.

[30] Smith and Carlson, *The Gift of Music: Great Composers and Their Influence*, 107.

[31] Krull, *Lives of the Musicians: Good Times, Bad Times*, 42.

[32] Smith and Carlson, *The Gift of Music: Great Composers and Their Influence*, 104.

[33] Krull, *Lives of the Musicians: Good Times, Bad Times*, 42.

[34] Smith and Carlson, *The Gift of Music: Great Composers and Their Influence*, 108.

[35] Brockway and Weinstock, *Men of Music: Their Lives, Times, and Achievements*, 304.

[36] Smith and Carlson, *The Gift of Music: Great Composers and Their Influence*, 105.

[37] Brockway and Weinstock, *Men of Music: Their Lives, Times, and Achievements*, 306.

[38] Bedford, *Robert Schumann: His Life and Work*, 173.

[39] Brockway and Weinstock, *Men of Music: Their Lives, Times, and Achievements*, 308.

[40] Ibid., 309.

[41] Smith and Carlson, *The Gift of Music: Great Composers and Their Influence*, 108.

[42] Brockway and Weinstock, *Men of Music: Their Lives, Times, and Achievements*, 308.

[43] Grew, *Masters of Music*, 257.

[44] Smith and Carlson, *The Gift of Music: Great Composers and Their Influence*, 108.

[45] Krull, *Lives of the Musicians: Good Times, Bad Times*, 43.